For Amelie, my beautiful mermaid, and all her lovely friends,
especially Roman and Sylvia.
May your dreams be as wide and vast as the sea.
C.B.

For Nanny Lyn, Granddad Terry & (not forgetting) Alfie!
Thank you for all the delicious cakes, and being so incredibly
supportive throughout my career. Lots of love, Lolly xxx
L.E.A.

First published in 2015 by Scholastic Children's Books
Euston House, 24 Eversholt Street
London NW1 1DB
a division of Scholastic Ltd
www.scholastic.co.uk
London ~ New York ~ Toronto ~ Sydney ~ Auckland
Mexico City ~ New Delhi ~ Hong Kong

Text copyright © 2015 Cerrie Burnell
Illustrations copyright © 2015 Laura Ellen Anderson

HB ISBN 978 1407 14592 1
PB ISBN 978 1407 14593 8

Mermaid

Written by **Cerrie Burnell**

Illustrated by **Laura Ellen Anderson**

SCHOLASTIC

Once there was a boy called Luka who lived by the shore of a deep silvery sea. Luka longed to splash in the surf and dive beneath the cool water, but he couldn't swim.

Nor could anyone in Luka's family. And they didn't understand his dream. "Why do you want to swim?" they asked. "The sea is cold and wild."

Then one day Luka saw a girl bobbing on the waves.
He gasped as she dipped and soared like a fish.

The girl swam to the edge of the pier. "Help me out, Dad!" she called, and her dad scooped her up and gently sat her in a wheelchair. "Thank you, Daddy," she laughed.

Luka hardly noticed the wheels of her chair – all he saw was the light of her smile and the power of the sea in her eyes.

Luka ran over to say hello. "I wish I could swim like you," he beamed.
"Hello, I'm Sylvia," giggled the girl. "I could teach you to swim."
Luka's heart beat with wonder.
His dream might really come true.

The next day, Luka put on his shorts and raced all the way to the sea.

There was Sylvia with her dad on the pier, her smile as bright as the sun.

"I'm in the sea!" Luka yelled as they splashed into the shallows.
Sylvia showed him how to paddle with his hands and kick with his legs.

And by the end of the day,
Luka could keep afloat by himself.

When the first stars began to sparkle, Luka said goodbye.
As he waved to Sylvia, moonlight glinted on her skin and for
a moment her legs looked like a tail that shone and glistened
like pearls. "Is she magical?" he wondered.

When Luka got home, his brothers
could not believe he'd been swimming.
"Wow," they whispered.
Luka felt like a king.

That night, Luka dreamed he was swimming underwater. Something was shimmering, lighting the way like a moon behind clouds.

Luka dived deeper and saw...

...Sylvia – with a beautiful tail!

"You're a mermaid," gasped Luka.
"Yes," smiled Sylvia, and she took his hand.

They glided through the waves together, laughing at jellyfish and darting between sea flowers. Sylvia tickled an octopus and Luka found an ancient treasure chest.

Then they arrived at a palace beneath the sea and both of them were still. It was the most magnificent sight Luka had ever seen.

"This used to be my home," said Sylvia softly.
"Why did you leave?" Luka asked.
"I dreamed of seeing the sun rise and hearing the birds
sing, of catching an autumn leaf and watching the snow fall."

As Sylvia spoke Luka saw that her dreams were as wide and vast as the sea, and that she was brave enough to go after them. And he realised that all of his dreams were possible too, as long as he dared to follow them.

When Luka awoke the next morning, his heart ever so gently ached. He missed Sylvia.

But when he got to school,
there was a big surprise:
a new girl was joining his class…
and it was Sylvia!

The other children crowded around her. "Where are you from?"
they asked.

"From far away," smiled Sylvia.

"Why are you in a wheelchair?" they murmured.

"Because she's a mermaid!" cried Luka,
"and she comes from a palace beneath the sea."

And Luka knew that to him she would always be a mermaid, and they would have a thousand more adventures together, watching the sun rise and the snow fall and diving through the waves of the deep silvery sea.